APPLE CIDER MAKING DAYS

APPLE CIDER MAKING DAYS

ANN PURMELL

Pictures by Joanne Friar

THE MILLBROOK PRESS
Brookfield, Connecticut

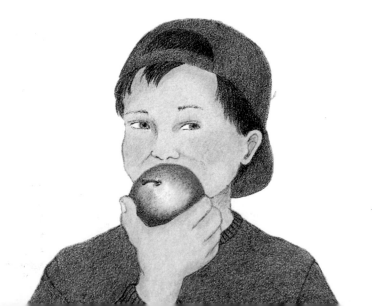

To my husband, Bruce, whose love of cider mills inspired me
to write this book. A.P.

To Donald, for all his support and four wonderful children—
Christopher, James, Elizabeth, and Mary. With love, J.F.

Published by The Millbrook Press, Inc.
2 Old New Milford Road
Brookfield, Connecticut 06804
www.millbrookpress.com

Library of Congress Cataloging-in-Publication Data
Purmell, Ann.
Apple cider making days / by Ann Purmell ; illustrated by
Joanne Friar.
p. cm.
Summary: Alex and Abigail join the whole family in pro-
cessing and selling apples and apple cider at their grand-
father's farm.
ISBN 0-7613-2364-3 (lib. bdg.)
[1. Apples—Harvesting—Fiction. 2. Apples—Fiction. 3.
Farm life—Fiction.] I. Friar, Joanne H., ill. II. Title.
PZ7.P977 Ap 2002   [E]—dc21   2001044920

Printed in the United States of America
4 5 3

Grandpa drives the tractor that pulls the wagon
that carries Alex and Abigail and all the aunts,
uncles, and cousins. It is fall, and these are cider-
making days on Grandpa's apple farm.

Grandpa grows dwarf apple trees that are about as tall as a person. Alex and Abigail pick apples from the lower branches with the cousins. The grown-ups pick the apples growing near the tops of the trees.

Alex and Abigail each take a handle and carry their wooden bushel basket full of apples to the wagon. Together they hoist the basket of bright red apples into the wagon.

When the wagon is full, Grandpa drives the
tractor to the barn. Alex and Abigail bump along
on a bench over the apples in the wagon.

Grandpa backs the wagon into the barn until it stands in front of the apple sorter. Alex and Abigail jump down. Grandpa and Abigail unload the apples into the sorter barrel.

Cousins run into the barn and take their places along the conveyor belt beside Alex and Abigail. Grandpa flips the sorter switch to "on." The sorting machine roars as loud as an airplane inside the barn. The conveyor belt moves along, and apples fall onto it from the barrel. Alex and Abigail and the cousins sort the perfect apples from the not-so-perfect apples.

The perfect apples move along toward the showers, where a spray of water washes them clean. They tumble across soft foam-padded rubber rollers that gently dry them. Aunts and uncles take the clean, dry, shiny apples and bag them to sell. They carry the bags to the cold-storage room. It is always about 40° F (4° C) inside. Brrr! These are called eating apples.

Alex and Abigail and the cousins toss the apples that are bruised or oddly shaped onto another conveyor belt for cider. The cider apples travel in a straight line up a slant as steep as a ski slope before they drop down into a grater with sharp metal blades. There they are chopped into small pieces, which Grandpa calls apple mush.

The apple mush is sucked up through wide bendable tubing. The uncles lay a steel frame under the cider press. They cover it with a clean burlap cloth. When the cloth is flat, Grandpa squirts gallons and gallons of apple mush onto it.

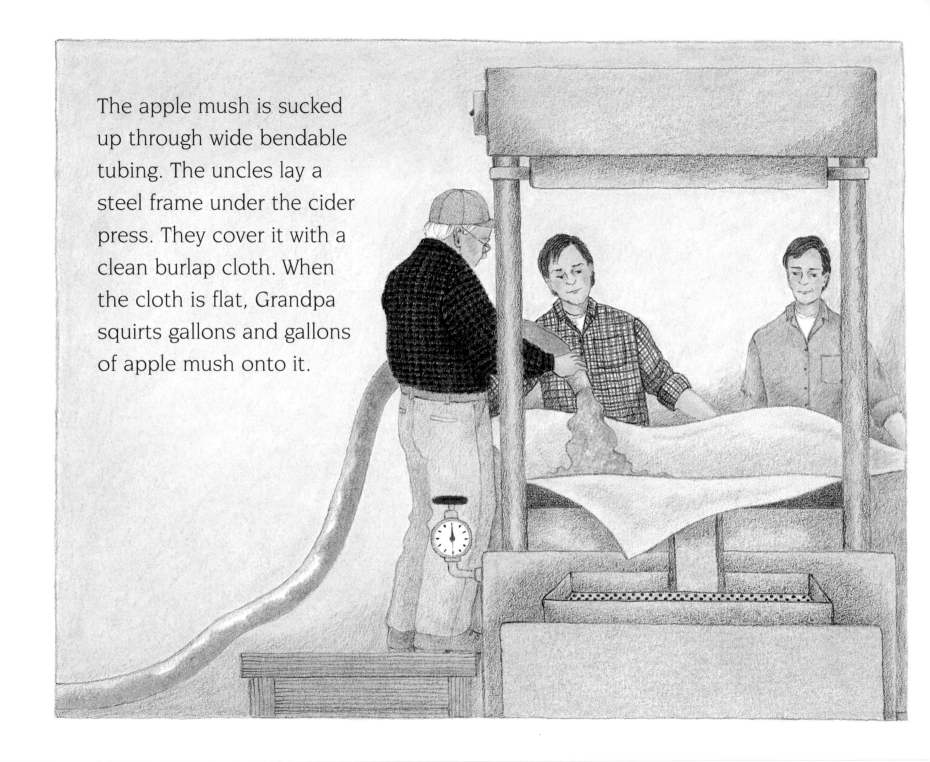

After the cloth is full, the uncles fold it so the sides meet in the middle. They set a heavy rack on top.

They repeat these steps until a huge pile of frames, cloths full of apple mush, and racks are piled on top of one another. Then Grandpa slowly lowers the pancake-flat steel plate of the cider press. This plate squeezes the cider juice out of the apple mush. As more and more pressure is exerted, the pile gets thinner. The air is filled with a strong sweet apple smell. At last, the golden-brown liquid begins to flow through clear tubing into a giant-sized steel holding tank. The cider is cooled and stored here until it is needed to fill jugs for people to buy.

Tomorrow, Grandpa will push open the heavy wooden door to The Apple Barn. He will crank the red-and-white-striped awning down until it spreads across the doorway. Then The Apple Barn will be open for business.

Many cars will park along the long gravel-covered drive that leads to The Apple Barn. City people will drive out into the country to buy jugs of Grandpa's cider, bags of eating apples, and Grandma's homemade doughnuts.

Tomorrow, Alex, Abigail, the aunts, uncles, and cousins will work hard all day long, waiting on people in the store, running warm doughnuts down from the farmhouse, pulling bags of apples from the cold-storage room, and keeping the cider flowing.

HOMEMADE JAM ~ HONEY

PLEASE ORDER
YOUR
THANKSGIVING
PIES
BY NOV. 20TH

6 75

2/$1

CANDY
APPLES
$1.00

PIES
AND
DONUTS

BITTERSWEET

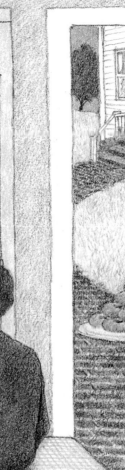

100% PURE APPLE CIDER

GALLONS + ½ GALLONS

ACORN SQUASH

BUTTERNUT

Today is the best cider-making day of all. It is the day Alex and Abigail, aunts, uncles, cousins, Grandpa, and Grandma drink the first sweet cider—the cider they all helped to make.

CIDER LORE

Cider makers use good-quality apples that are not a perfect shape or color. They do not use ground-fallen or rotten apples because these would ruin the flavor of cider.

●

The dark amber color of cider is from apple solids such as pulp. Apple juice has no solids so it is pale yellow.

●

Cider is a combination of sweet and tart apples, usually three to five varieties. Many cider makers keep their blend of apples a secret.

●

No two pressings of cider taste the same. The amount of sugar in apples changes constantly, which makes the flavor of each batch different even if the same blend of apples is used each time.

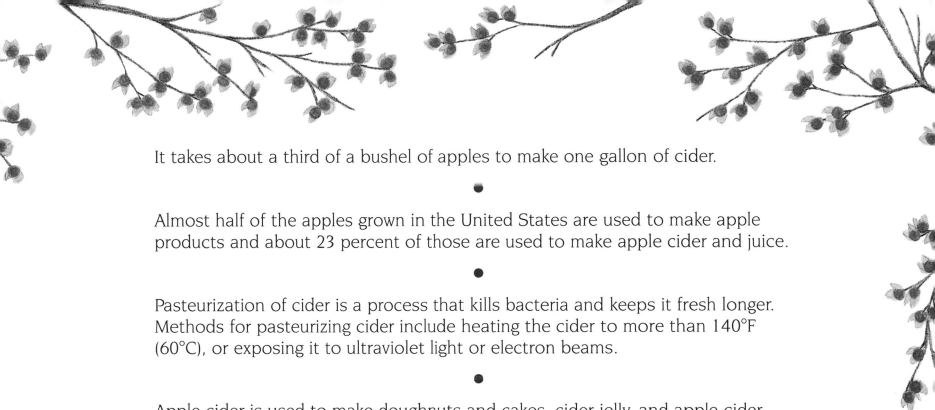

It takes about a third of a bushel of apples to make one gallon of cider.

•

Almost half of the apples grown in the United States are used to make apple products and about 23 percent of those are used to make apple cider and juice.

•

Pasteurization of cider is a process that kills bacteria and keeps it fresh longer. Methods for pasteurizing cider include heating the cider to more than 140°F (60°C), or exposing it to ultraviolet light or electron beams.

•

Apple cider is used to make doughnuts and cakes, cider jelly, and apple cider vinegar—even apple cider ice-cream sodas.

•

October is National Apple Month. Enjoy a glass of cold cider!

ACKNOWLEDGMENTS

With heartfelt thanks to everyone who helped me along the way:

Margaret Beison, the best children's librarian and manuscript reader.

David Burns and the Spring Arbor University Library.

Jack Esterline, my cheerleader.

Ray Meckley, who allowed me free run of his cider press room at Flavor Fruit Farms.

John Piper, Editor, *Jackson Citizen Patriot* newspaper, who gave me my start.

Kristy Michaels and Libby Rehor, for countless hours of babysitting.

Laurence Pringle and Jane Yolen, for their friendship in writing.

Jean Reynolds, my editor, who had the vision to publish this book.